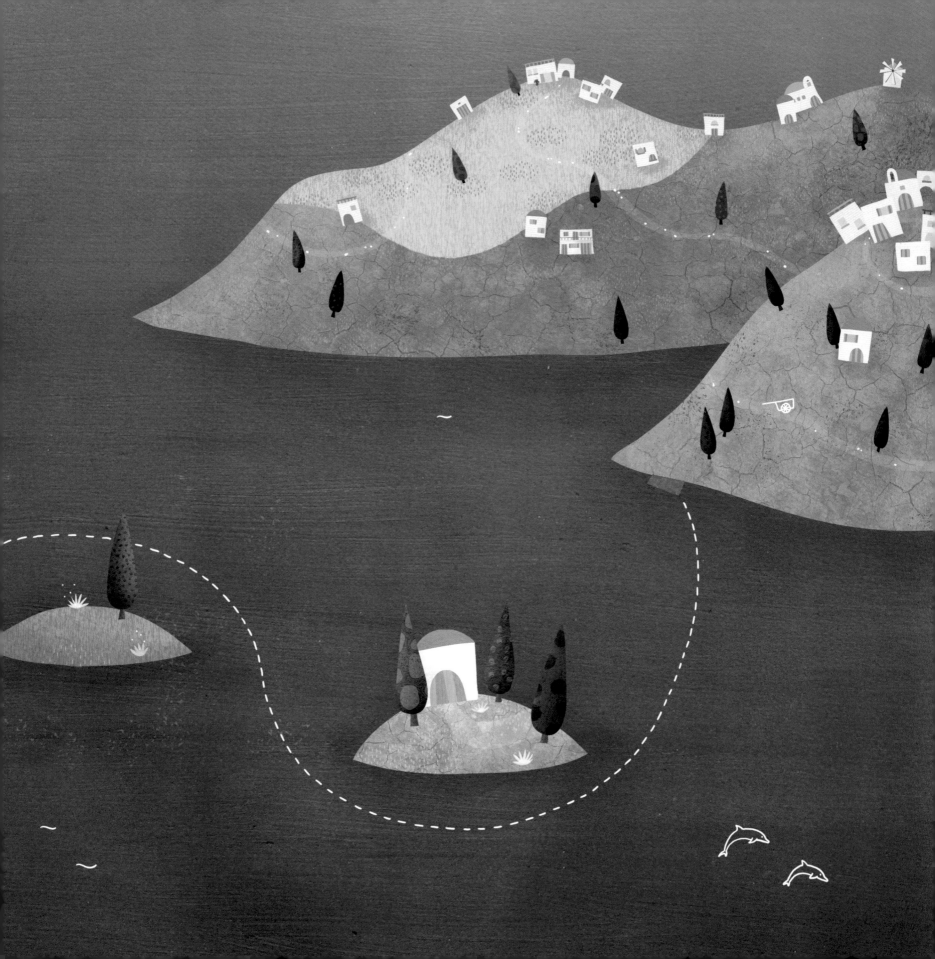

Published by Top That! Publishing plc
Tide Mill Way, Woodbridge, Suffolk, IP12 1AP, UK
www.topthatpublishing.com
Text copyright © Nicole Snitselaar 2011
Illustrations copyright © Coralie Saudo 2011
All rights reserved
0 2 4 6 8 9 7 5 3 1
Printed and bound in China

Creative Director – Simon Couchman
Editorial Director – Daniel Graham

Illustrated by Coralie Saudo
Written by Nicole Snitselaar

ISBN 978-1-84956-245-4

A catalogue record for this book is available from the British Library
Printed and bound in China

Little Grey Donkey

Illustrated by Coralie Saudo
Written by Nicole Snitselaar

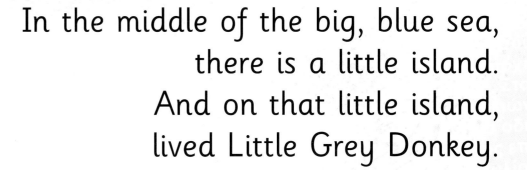

In the middle of the big, blue sea,
there is a little island.
And on that little island,
lived Little Grey Donkey.

Every day, a little girl called Sérafina came to visit Little Grey Donkey. She always brought some nice crunchy carrots and they enjoyed playing together in the shade of the green cypress trees.

But one day, Sérafina did not
come and visit Little Grey Donkey!
No crunchy carrots, no games,
no loving words whispered in his ear.
Little Grey Donkey was very upset.

Little Grey Donkey waited
and waited for Sérafina to arrive.
Many bright mornings and dark nights followed.
'Where is Sérafina? Why doesn't she come?'
wondered Little Grey Donkey.
Little Grey Donkey was worried about Sérafina,
and so he decided to go and look for her.

The path Little Grey Donkey followed
was very narrow and terribly steep!
'I can't go on! I'm too scared,' cried Little Grey Donkey.
Then he remembered Sérafina, swallowed his fears, and
bravely started down the track.

Further along, Little Grey Donkey discovered a skateboard at the edge of a very steep cliff. 'This cliff is too steep. I'm going to fall and hurt myself!' cried Little Grey Donkey. Then he remembered Sérafina, swallowed his fears, sat on the skateboard and raced down the slope.

Once Little Grey Donkey
reached the bottom of the
cliff, he discovered that the
only way to go further was
to climb into a small boat.
'Me? In a boat? I'm much
too scared to do that!'
cried Little Grey Donkey.
Then he remembered Sérafina,
swallowed his fears and got
into the boat.

Using all of his strength, Little Grey Donkey rowed across
the sea and discovered a small village perched on
the top of the cliffs.
'Must I use this rusty brown lift? Never!
I might fall down or get stuck,' cried Little Grey Donkey.
Then he remembered Sérafina, swallowed his fears,
climbed on the lift and was hoisted to the top.

Still trembling with fright, Little Grey Donkey
stepped out onto the cobbled street.
'What a dangerous journey! How can Sérafina
do it every day?' wondered Little Grey Donkey.
Little Grey Donkey walked through the streets
calling Sérafina's name. Then he met a boy.
'You're Sérafina's Little Grey Donkey!
Come with me. I know where she lives!'

Καλημέρα

81

Σεραφι

Sérafina had been ill and was resting on the rooftop terrace of her house. 'Little Grey Donkey! You came all this way to visit me,' she cried with surprise.

'How did you manage it?' asked Sérafina.
Sérafina knew all about the narrow
mountain track, the steep cliff, the boat,
and the rusty lift.
Little Grey Donkey smiled up at Sérafina.
'I thought of you, swallowed my fears,
and was filled with …

Φιλία

… love.'

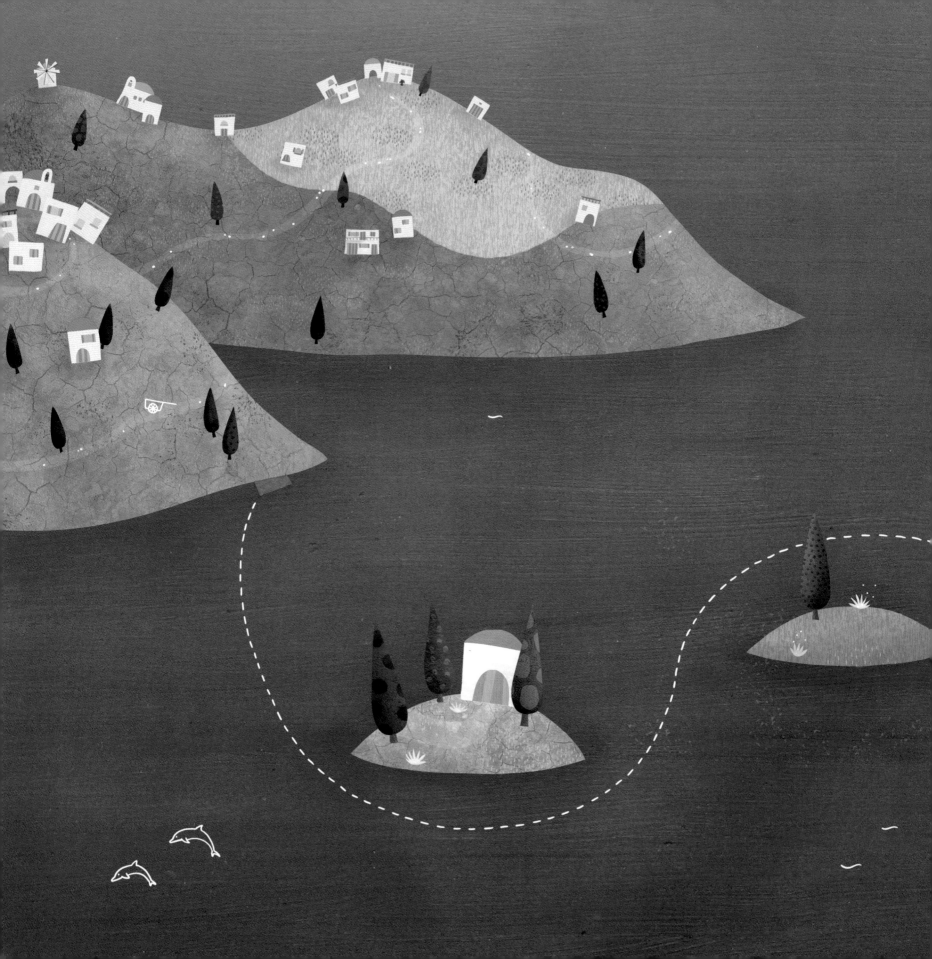

More great picture books from Top That! Publishing

ISBN 978-1-84956-120-4

Baby Bear tentatively explores the wonders of the outside world.

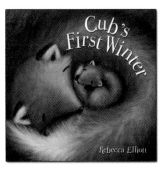

ISBN 978-1-84956-099-3

An inquisitive fox cub experiences the onset of his first winter.

ISBN 978-1-84956-303-1

Snuffletrump the piglet will try anything to get rid of his hiccups!

ISBN 978-1-84956-073-3

Can you find Hiku as he sneaks away from an important family visit?

ISBN 978-1-84956-305-5

The animals are making a hullabaloo in this humorous picture storybook!

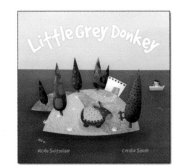

ISBN 978-1-84956-245-4

Unique illustrations capture the loving bond between two best friends!

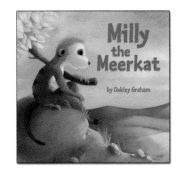

ISBN 978-1-84956-304-8

Milly the meerkat learns a very important lesson in this classic tale.

ISBN 978-1-84956-302-4

Follow the antics of the escaped zoo animals as they cause pandamonium!

ISBN 978-1-84956-101-3

Enjoy the beautiful moments between a mother cat and her kitten.

ISBN 978-1-84956-100-6

Comic wordplay explores what a toucan or toucan't do.

Available from all good bookstores or visit www.topthatpublishing.com
Look for Top That! Apps on the Apple iTunes Store